# Time to Sleep,
# Alfie Bear!

## Catherine Walters

**LITTLE TIGER PRESS**
London

"It's nearly bedtime, Alfie," called Mother Bear, gathering up his baby brother and sister.

"It can't be bedtime," Alfie complained. "It's still light."

"It's always light at bedtime in the summer," said Mother Bear. "Come along – it's bath time."

Alfie sat by the edge of the lake.
The fish leaped to catch the evening flies.
 "Huh! The fish aren't going to bed,"
thought Alfie. "Why should I?"
 It gave him an idea . . .

"Look! I'm a fish!" shouted Alfie. "I don't have to go to bed!"

He began to jump and dive and splash. The babies laughed and splashed too. "Don't do that," sighed Mother Bear. "The babies are getting too excited to sleep."

When they had all calmed down,
Mother Bear took them back home.
"It's a warm night," she said.
"Go and get some nice, cool
grass for bedding, Alfie. That
will help you sleep."

Alfie went outside and pulled
up a few pawfuls of grass.
   Some owls were swooping through
the meadow.
   "The owls aren't going to bed,"
thought Alfie. "Why should I?"

Alfie rushed back into the cave and began to flap his arms. "Look! I'm an owl!" he hooted. "I don't need to go to bed."

"Oh, Alfie, stop that!" groaned Mother Bear. "Look, the babies are throwing all their lovely bedding around, too. None of you will have anywhere to sleep."

At last, Alfie and the babies were safely in bed.
"I think you need a nice, gentle song," said
Mother Bear. "Now, close your eyes."
Alfie wasn't listening. Outside, he
could hear wolves howling.
"The wolves aren't going to sleep,"
he thought. "Why should I?"

"Look, I'm a wolf! AAAAOOOW!" said Alfie.
"OW, OW, OW!" shrieked the babies.
"That's enough, Alfie," Mother Bear
growled. "I don't want any little wolves
in the cave. You can wait outside until the
babies are asleep."

"Hooray!" cried Alfie, running outside.

He charged across the meadow, howling, "AAAAOOOW!"

Then, from somewhere close by, someone answered him, "AAAAOOOW!"

Alfie jumped. There in front of him was
a wolf cub, with his family close by.
 "Are you a wolf?" the cub asked.
"You sound like one, but you don't look
like one."
 "Are you sure you're a wolf?" called
a big, gruff voice . . .

"...because you look like a little bear to me!"
    It was Father Bear.
    "I'm a bear, I'm a bear!" shouted Alfie,
as Father Bear picked him up.
    "Goodnight, little bear," the wolf
cub called.

"So you're a bear?" Father Bear said.
"But are you a sleepy bear all ready for bed?"
    "No," said Alfie. "I'm not—"
    But before he could finish speaking,
he had fallen fast asleep.

*To our little Jubilee boy,*
*Frankie*
*~ C W*

LITTLE TIGER PRESS
1 The Coda Centre, 189 Munster Road, London SW6 6AW
www.littletiger.co.uk

First published in Great Britain 2003
This edition published 2012

Printed in China • LTP/1800/0794/0913
4 6 8 10 9 7 5 3

Alfie Bear doesn't want to go to bed. He's not sleepy at all! The fish and the owls and the wolves are all still awake, and Alfie wants to stay up and splash and swoop and howl too! In fact, he is determined to stay awake for ever . . .